W9-CAM-983

Stolen Stash

By Sally Rippin

A DIVISION OF EDC PUBLISHING

Chapter One

Billie and her friends sit in their classroom on Monday morning in silence. Everyone in the class faces the front, staring at Mr. Benetto, whose face is as dark as a storm cloud. He has just told them the most terrible news.

Something has been taken from the principal's office. And Mrs. Singh thinks it was someone from the school!

"This is a very serious matter," Mr. Benetto says, his usually smiley face crinkled into a frown. "Mrs. Singh is very disappointed, but she is hoping that the person who did this will own up."

There is **shuffling** and **murmuring** as Billie's classmates slide their eyes from side to side.

Could the thief be in this very room? Billie wonders.

She is finding it hard not to feel a teensy bit **excited**, even though she knows a terrible thing has happened. The theft means there might be a mystery to uncover. Could it be a job for the Secret Mystery Club? If so, it might be their most serious yet!

She glances over at Jack, but his eyes are fixed on Mr. Benetto's serious face.

Even though, of course, Billie is hoping the person who stole the valuable thing confesses by the end of the day, there is a teensy part of her that hopes they don't. She would love to investigate and find out who did it, with the help of the SMC.

"All right then," Mr. Benetto says, his voice softening back to its usual tone. "Enough of the bad news. Let's get to work on our geography projects, shall we?"

5

Everyone starts chatting and moving around the classroom like normal again. They collect scissors and glue sticks and jars of colored pencils from the carts on the back wall, to continue working on their projects.

But Billie can't stop thinking about what Mr. Benetto has told them. She slides up next to Jack. "What do you think?" she whispers excitedly. "Is this our next mystery?"

Jack shrugs. "I don't know, Billie. It will probably all be over by the end of the day. Someone will own up, I'm sure."

"You're right," Billie says, nodding. "Of course that would be best."

But she crosses her fingers behind her back so Jack doesn't see. She can't help hoping that the SMC will be able to discover who the thief is.

All that day, Billie overhears people talking about the theft.

It is the most exciting thing that's happened at the school in months!

"What do you think was stolen?"

"Do you think someone will own up?"

"Who do you think it was?"

The school day is almost over. Mrs. Singh calls the whole school together for an assembly, just before the final bell goes. Whispers pass through the students like wind through the trees.

Everyone wants to know if the thief has owned up – especially Billie. Then she will know if the SMC has a new mystery to solve!

Chapter Two

"As you all know," Mrs. Singh begins, "something was taken from my office last Friday afternoon. And I am very disappointed that no one has come forward to return it."

The students murmur among themselves.

Mrs. Singh holds up a hand to silence them.

Carrie, the school president, puts her hand up. "Mrs. Singh, can you tell us what was stolen?" she asks.

Everyone in the whole school stares at her. Even if she is the school president, this seems like a very brave thing to ask.

Mrs. Singh pauses while she decides what to say. Mrs. Singh never wastes words.

"It was money from the school cash box, Carrie," Mrs. Singh says. "Mrs. Saunders from the front desk was counting the money in my office. She left the office for a moment to help someone to the nurse, and when she came back, someone had taken a fifty dollar bill from the cash box."

There are **gasps** from all over the hall. Even the little kindergarteners in the front row sit with their mouths gaping open like goldfish.

Stealing money! Billie thinks. *That's serious!*

"I still hope that whoever took the money might return it to my office," Mrs. Singh says. "I feel very sad that one of our students would do something like this. All right. That's enough for now. You may go."

The students shuffle out of the assembly hall, talking loudly about what has happened. They run to collect their bikes or meet their parents in the playground.

Billie and Jack find Mika and Alex in the crowd.

"So, what do you think?" Billie asks.

"It's terrible!" Mika says, shaking her head. "Imagine stealing money!"

"No, I mean, do you think this could be a job for the SMC?" Billie insists.

Alex narrows his eyes. "No way, Billie. What we do is games. This is serious. Didn't you see how cross Mrs. Singh was?"

16

"Games?" Billie **splutters**. She can't believe what she is hearing. "Is that what you think we're doing? Playing games? Well, I think the Secret Mystery Club is very serious. How many mysteries have we already solved?"

"Possum thieves?" Alex snorts. "Codes written by our parents? Witches who aren't really witches?" He rolls his eyes at Mika. "And don't forget criminals who put leaves in sandwiches."

Billie gasps. Alex's words feel like sharp spikes in her chest. Her head **fizzes** angrily. "Is that really what you think of the SMC?" she says in disbelief. "Well, I don't know why you bother hanging out with us then, Alex. If you think the club is so babyish, you should probably just leave."

"Maybe I will," says Alex, glaring at Billie.

"Maybe you should." Billie glares back.

"Billie," Mika says, "you don't mean that!" She puts her hand on Billie's arm. But Billie spins around and **storms** off towards the school gates, with Jack trailing behind her.

Chapter Three

"That Alex!" Billie fumes, as she and Jack make their way home. "We don't need him anyway! The SMC is much better off without him."

Jack chews the inside of his cheek nervously. Billie can see he's not quite sure what to say.

She kicks a pebble angrily into the gutter.

"Maybe he has a point, Billie," Jack says quietly. "Stealing money is a pretty serious crime. Maybe we shouldn't get involved."

Billie stops and spins around to face him. "Are you taking his side?" she demands.

"No!" Jack says, frowning. "I'm your best friend, aren't I? We always stick together."

"Sorry," says Billie. Jack is right. He always sticks by her, no matter what. She smiles gratefully. "Thanks, Jack."

When they reach Billie's front gate, she turns to Jack. "Do you want to come over?" she asks. "Dad made banana bread last night. We can eat some in the tree house and see if we can solve the mystery of who took the money."

Jack frowns. "Mmm, maybe later," he says. "I've got homework."

Billie nods, like she doesn't care. But she knows Jack doesn't want to talk about the mystery anymore, and this makes her feel like she has a little **bruise** inside her chest.

As soon as she is inside, she dumps her schoolbag at the bottom of the stairs, grabs some banana bread and races out back to climb up into the tree house.

I'll show them! she thinks. *I'll show them that I can solve big mysteries, all on my own.*

Billie drags some cushions into a pile and pulls out her secret notebook from its hiding place in a hole in the trunk of the tree. Then she settles down with her pen and notebook to write everything she knows about what's happened.

Secret Mystery Number 5

The Crime: Money was stolen from Mrs. Singh's office

The Time: Last Friday afternoon

Suspects: Everyone in the school!

Billie crosses the last sentence out.

That's way too many people to be suspects, she thinks. *I have to narrow it down somehow.*

What kind of person would steal money? she wonders.

She wishes Jack and Mika were around to help her. Even Alex. He can be annoying, but he is still very good at coming up with clues.

Billie sighs. It's no use. Detective work is no fun when you are on your own.

26

She locks her notebook up again with the tiny key and pushes it back into the hole in the tree trunk. Then she swings down out of the tree and **trudges** back inside.

Chapter Four

The next morning Billie and Jack walk to school together as usual and wait for Mika and Alex under the pepper tree. They wait and they wait, until eventually the bell goes. The two of them look around anxiously for their friends. Mika is often late, but it is strange that Alex hasn't turned up yet.

He usually arrives at school at the same time as Jack and Billie.

Jack frowns. "Maybe he's sick?" he suggests.

"Maybe," says Billie. "Come on, we can't wait any longer or we'll get in trouble with Mr. Benetto for being late."

Billie and Jack jog into the school building.

Everyone is already in their classrooms and the corridor is quiet and empty. As they pass Mrs. Singh's office, they hear voices coming from behind the door.

"Wait!" Billie whispers, grabbing Jack's arm to stop him. She glances up the corridor to check that no one is around, then puts her ear to the door. Jack chews his lip nervously but does the same.

They hear the sound of Mrs. Singh's voice, **stern** and **disappointed**.

"Well, I'm glad the money has been returned," she is saying. "Although I don't understand why you didn't come forward yesterday. I have no idea what made you do such a thing. I really hope I can expect better from you in the future."

The person Mrs. Singh is scolding mumbles something in answer.

Billie widens her eyes at Jack. "It's the thief!" she whispers.

Jack's mouth drops open. Billie flattens her ear to the door again.

"I will keep this between us," she hears Mrs. Singh continue, a little softer now. "I think you've been punished enough without your friends finding out what you've done. I'm sure they would be very disappointed in you. All right, you can go to class now."

Quickly, Billie and Jack **spring** away from the door and look around frantically for somewhere to hide. Billie grabs Jack's hand and pulls him into the entrance of the girls' bathroom.

They press themselves against the wall, out of sight. Billie's heart is **pounding** hard.

When they hear Mrs. Singh's door close again they peer around the doorway to try to catch a glimpse of the thief.

Billie feels her tummy **jump** around with excitement. *Who is it?* she wonders. *Who stole the money?*

They see the student walking down the corridor, head hung low. It's a boy – tall, thin and with dark hair.

As the boy turns to head out onto the playground, they catch a glimpse of his face before he disappears around the corner.

Billie clutches Jack's hand. She can't believe her eyes.

"Was that…?" Billie gasps.

Jack nods. "Alex!" he finishes for her, and they stare at each other, mouths open.

Chapter Five

"Alex is the thief?" Billie says as they run to their classroom.

Jack shakes his head in disbelief. "I can't believe it! *Alex?*"

All kinds of feelings **bubble** up inside Billie: shock, surprise and, last of all, anger.

"Well, that explains a lot!" she says, frowning. "Now I understand why he didn't want the SMC to investigate this mystery. He didn't want us to find out it was him!"

Billie and Jack get to class and sit down in their seats just as Mika and Alex walk in. Luckily, Mr. Benetto hasn't called the roll yet, so he doesn't notice how late they all are.

Billie glances at Alex as he pulls out his chair. His eyes are red and it looks like he's been crying.

Serves him right! Billie thinks angrily. *I can't believe that a member of the Secret Mystery Club is a thief!*

Billie sees Mika put a comforting hand on Alex's shoulder before she goes to her own seat.

Wait until you find out what he did, Mika! Billie thinks. *You won't feel so sorry for him then!*

"OK, kids," Mr. Benetto says. "I want you to try to finish off your geography projects today.

If you've already finished, you can join another group to help them out. You have until recess to get them done."

"I'll get the pencils and things, you get the poster," Billie tells Jack.

Jack nods and walks off to collect the half-finished poster he and Billie have been working on.

Billie walks to the back of the room to collect scissors and glue and colored pencils.

When she gets back to her desk, she is surprised to see Mika and Alex there.

"We've finished our project," Mika says, smiling, "so we thought we could help you with yours. Is that OK?"

Billie looks at Jack. He looks away, chewing on a thumbnail.

"I don't think so," Billie says **coolly**. "We can finish it ourselves. Thanks anyway."

41

Mika looks confused. "But you've still got heaps to do. And Mr. Benetto said Alex and I have to find someone to help."

"I told you," Billie says more firmly now. "We don't need your help."

"Billie! What's wrong with you?" asks Mika, **frowning**. "Why are you acting so strange? I know you and Alex had a fight, but you're still friends, aren't you?"

"Are we?" Billie says, glaring at Alex.

"Friends are people you can trust. Friends are people who stick by you. I don't think you should be his friend either, Mika, if you want to stay a member of the SMC."

Alex's cheeks turn red. Mika's eyes grow wide and she puts her hands on her hips. She doesn't get angry very often, but when she does, she gets very angry indeed.

"That's not what our club is about, Billie," Mika **hisses**. "I'm not going to choose sides. If that's how you are going to be, then I don't want to be a member of the club anyway!"

Billie's mouth falls open. She didn't think Mika would take Alex's side. "But Mika, you were my friend first!" she says in disbelief. "Besides, you don't know what Alex did…"

"Billie!" Jack says suddenly, so loudly that even Mr. Benetto notices.

"Kids!" Mr. Benetto says in a stern voice. "Is that geography you're talking about?"

"No," says Mika, pulling Alex away from Billie's desk. "Alex and I are just trying to find someone who'd like some help. Billie and Jack don't need us."

"We need some help!" Benny says quickly, shooting up his hand.

"All right, off you go then, Mika and Alex," Mr. Benetto says.

"Billie, Jack, heads down now.
I want your project on my desk
by recess."

Billie ducks her head down over
her work. When she looks up again,
Jack is glaring at her angrily.

"What?" she whispers, feeling her
throat get **tight**. "He's the one in the
wrong, Jack! You're not going to
take his side, too, are you?"

Jack shakes his head. "No," he says.
"Like I said, you're my best friend.

46

But that wasn't fair what you did just now. I don't think we should tell anyone else about what Alex did. Mrs. Singh said he'd been punished enough."

Billie sticks out her bottom lip. She knows Jack is right, but she still feels angry and confused. This isn't what was supposed to happen! Alex is the one who did the bad thing, but now she's the one everyone is angry at! This is **not fair**. Not at all!

Chapter Six

Billie and Jack just finish their project as the bell rings for recess. They stay for a minute to tidy up, then run out onto the playground.

The sun is shining so brightly that Billie almost forgets about her argument with Alex and Mika.

That is, until she sees Mika sitting by herself under the pepper tree. Alex is nowhere to be seen.

"Come on," says Jack. "Let's go and see if she's OK."

Billie **hesitates**, but only for a second. Then she runs after Jack.

Mika looks up at Billie and narrows her eyes. But Billie has already practiced in her head what she is going to say. She doesn't want to lose Mika as a friend.

And she especially doesn't want the Secret Mystery Club to be over!

"I'm sorry I was mean to you and Alex, Mika. It's just that…"

"Alex has gone home," Mika says. "He's not feeling well."

"Oh," says Billie, feeling a little worried. Even if he is a thief, Billie doesn't want anything really bad to happen to Alex. "What's wrong?"

"He knows you think he stole the money, Billie," Mika says.

Billie looks at Jack. He shrugs.

"But he didn't," Mika frowns.

"Well," says Billie slowly, "we actually saw him come out of Mrs. Singh's office. And we heard her telling him off for it. He definitely took the money, Mika." She looks at Mika, expecting her to be **horrified**, but instead Mika just looks angry.

"Billie," Mika snaps, "Alex is our friend. You know he wouldn't do a thing like that! He's not a thief!"

Billie looks back at Jack, who frowns. "I agree with Mika, Billie," he says. "Alex is our friend. He's a member of our club. He wouldn't do a thing like that."

Billie can't believe it. "But we saw him come out of Mrs. Singh's office!" she insists. "And we heard her telling him off."

"True," Jack says. "But there could still be another explanation. He might know who took the money, even if he didn't take it himself."

53

Billie gasps. "You mean he might be covering for someone?"

Mika and Jack nod.

"You are enough of a detective to know that a case isn't always as simple as it looks," Jack says.

Billie's stomach drops. She has been an awful friend to Alex. She knows him well enough to believe that Mika and Jack are right.

"You're right," she says, ashamed. "Alex wouldn't steal money."

Billie feels bad that she ever doubted Alex. She knows he is much too honest to steal.

All of the horrible mixed-up feelings disappear and an excited little **wriggle** creeps back into Billie's tummy. She looks at her friends. "So if he didn't do it," she says, grinning, "who did?"

"Well, there's still three of us left in the Secret Mystery Club." Mika smiles. "I reckon that should be enough to solve this mystery."

Billie grins, and she and Jack slap their hands down on Mika's. They all crow loudly. "Cock-a-doodle-doooooo!"

Billie is determined to get to the bottom of this. Of course she wants the SMC to solve the mystery, but most of all she wants to make it up to Alex. It's up to her to put things right.

Chapter Seven

That afternoon, when she gets home from school, Billie takes a clean sheet of paper and her sparkly pens out of her desk drawer. She folds the paper in half and draws a picture of a funny face on the front. Then she writes inside the card.

Dear Alex,

I'm sorry I was mean to you and I'm sorry you're sick now. Get better soon because we miss you at school. Me especially.

From,
Billie

Then Billie goes downstairs to find her mom, taking her card with her. Billie's mom is in the garden with Noah. She is planting tiny lettuce plants in the vegetable patch. Noah is making mud pies. There is dirt and water everywhere!

Noah looks up at Billie and smiles.

"Chocolate cake?" he says, holding up a handful of mud.

"No, thanks!" Billie giggles. "Mom, would it be OK if I rode my bike over to see Alex?" she asks.
"He went home sick today and I want to take him a card."

"Sure," Billie's mom says. "Is Jack going with you?"

Billie looks over the fence towards Jack's house.

60

"Nah, I think I'll go by myself," she says.

"OK, but be back by dinner," Billie's mom says, scraping a blob of mud out of Noah's hair.

"I will!" says Billie, grabbing her bike and hopping on.

Billie reaches Alex's house in record time. His mom lets Billie in and shows her to the back room, where Alex and his brother are playing on their PlayStation.

Billie **hovers** in the doorway for a moment, feeling nervous.

Will Alex still be mad at me? she wonders. She takes a **deep** breath. *I hope he'll still want to be my friend.*

"Hey, Alex," she says. "I just came over to see how you're feeling."

Alex turns around and looks surprised to see Billie standing there. But then, instead of getting angry, he looks happy to see her. Very happy, in fact.

"Hey! Thanks, Billie," he says, smiling.

"Hi, Billie!" Alex's little brother, Simon, says. He runs up to give Billie a hug.

Simon is only a bit older than Noah, but he started school this year. Every time he sees Billie in the playground he runs up to hug her.

"Hey, Slimy!" Billie says, like she always does. She tickles him and he giggles.

"Come and play!" Simon says. "You can have my turn. I'm winning!"

Alex gives Billie a look, which she recognizes as saying: "Only because I'm letting him!"

"OK, but I have to be home for dinner," Billie says.

She sits down next to Alex and picks up Simon's console.

"So, you don't look very sick," she jokes, handing Alex the card she made. She watches him read it.

When he's finished reading, Alex gives her a smile that lets her know that everything is OK between them again. "Thanks, Billie," he says. Billie breathes out a sigh of relief.

"My teacher is sick, too!" Simon says. "Everyone in the class made her a card, but I wanted to get her a present. But I didn't have enough money. So, I…"

"You made her a good card," Alex interrupts, putting his hand on his brother's arm and glaring at him.

Simon gets a funny look on his face. He hangs his head like a puppy that has just been scolded.

Billie feels a little **shiver** pass through her. She thinks she has just gotten the clue she needed. Everything **clicks** into place.

Billie stays for one more game, then rides home before it gets dark. She doesn't stop smiling the whole way there. Now she is sure she knows who stole the money!

Chapter Eight

The next morning Billie calls
an emergency SMC meeting
underneath the pepper tree before
school. For once Mika is on time.
She and Jack huddle close and
listen to everything Billie has
to say.

"But why wouldn't Alex just tell Mrs. Singh it was his little brother who took the money?" Jack asks.

Billie shrugs. "Maybe he's trying to protect him. That's what big brothers and sisters do."

Mika and Jack look at each other. Neither of them have brothers or sisters, so they know they can only take Billie's word on this.

"If that's the case, that's a pretty nice thing to do," Mika says.

Billie nods. "It is. That's why we have to find a way to tell Mrs. Singh it wasn't Alex without her finding out it's us. After all, we can't let her know we were listening at her door. But it's not fair that Alex should be punished for something he didn't do."

Jack nods. "I just found out from Lola, who found out from Poppy's sister, that as his punishment, Alex is not allowed to go to school camp."

"Really?" Mika **gasps**. "But that's terrible! We have to help him. He can't miss out on camp!"

"No way!" says Billie.

"So what do we do?" asks Jack.

Billie grins. She has had an idea. A super-duper idea. "We write Mrs. Singh an anonymous letter. That way no one will ever know it was us."

"Awesome idea!" says Jack. "Let's do it right away. Has anyone got a pen and paper on them?"

Billie smiles. "Always!" she says, pulling her secret notebook and sparkly pens out of her schoolbag.

She rips a page out of the book and quickly writes the note. She tries to **disguise** her handwriting, just in case.

The three of them walk to Mrs. Singh's office together. When they are sure no one is looking, they slip the note under Mrs. Singh's door and run to class, sliding into their seats just before the bell rings.

Alex is already at his desk and Billie gives him a little wave. He smiles and waves back. Billie feels good knowing that they are friends again.

Chapter Nine

That morning, Billie's class has a math test, then spelling. Billie and her friends are too busy with work to chat about the note, but Billie hasn't stopped thinking about it. She hopes so much that it will put things right.

Billie looks at the clock. Finally!
It is almost recess time.

But just then, only a minute
before the bell goes, there is an
announcement over the intercom.
"Would these four students please
go to Mrs. Singh's office at recess:
Billie, Jack, Mika and Alex."

Billie looks at her friends with
wide eyes. They look back at her,
as horrified as she feels. Alex
looks the most horrified of all.

The bell rings and everyone watches as the four friends put away their things and walk out of the room. Billie hears the whispers as she walks past. Only people who are in **big trouble** get called to the principal's office!

They walk slowly down the corridor, too worried to even talk to each other. When they reach the principal's office they pause at her door. Jack, Mika and Alex look at Billie.

This is all my fault! Billie thinks. She takes a deep breath, then knocks on the door. *What trouble have I gotten my friends into now?*

"Come in!" Mrs. Singh calls.

Billie opens the office door. There are four chairs lined up in front of the desk, and they each sit down in one of them. Right away, Billie sees her note on Mrs. Singh's desk, and her stomach **crumples**.

Mrs. Singh picks up the paper.

"Would anyone like to tell me about this?" she says, raising one eyebrow.

Jack and Mika look at Billie. Alex just looks confused. Billie sighs. Then she takes another deep breath. There is no way out except to tell the truth.

"We found out that you thought that Alex took the money from the cash box," she begins. "But then we also found out that it wasn't him."

She turns and looks at Alex apologetically. He has a funny look on his face.

"We think he was trying to cover for his little brother," Billie continues. "But we didn't want him to be punished for something he didn't do. We didn't want him to miss out on school camp. That would be awful! But we also didn't want him to know that we knew…" Billie drifts off into a mumble. She knows how jumbled her explanation sounds.

80

"Billie!" says Alex, sounding annoyed.

"It wasn't just Billie's idea!" Jack jumps in. "It was Mika and me, too!"

Billie feels Mika's hand on her shoulder and a warm rush of gratitude flows through her.
My friends are the best! she thinks.

When Billie looks up again, she is surprised to see a small smile on Mrs. Singh's face.

"Well, you four are certainly a team, aren't you?" Mrs. Singh says. "Alex, you stuck up for your brother. Billie, you stuck up for Alex. And then Jack and Mika, you stuck up for Billie. It makes me very happy to see my students stand up for what they believe in."

There is a short pause as Billie and her friends take in what Mrs. Singh has said.

"Really?" Billie says finally. "You mean we're not in trouble?"

Mrs. Singh shakes her head.

"What about Simon?" Alex asks nervously.

"Well, Alex, I will still need to speak to your little brother about what he did," Mrs. Singh says. "I know he's only little, but he needs to understand that what he did was very wrong."

"He just wanted to buy a present for his teacher!" Alex explains. "He asked if he could borrow some money from me. I should have said yes.

Then he wouldn't have taken it from the office." Alex sighs. "He didn't understand that it was stealing, Mrs. Singh. He said the money was just there and that there was plenty more in the box. He didn't even think anyone would notice."

"But he understands now?" Mrs. Singh says.

Alex nods. "I explained it to him. He's very sorry."

"You're a good brother," Mrs. Singh says. "And the four of you make a good team. Not just great friends but also great detectives, I believe?"

Billie looks up at Mrs. Singh in surprise. "But…but… How do you know…?" she stammers.

Mrs. Singh smiles. "I was a bit of a detective myself at your age," she says. "I haven't lost my skills. I know, for instance, that you have a set of **sparkly** pens, Billie, as well as a very small notebook.

This note here is written on very small paper. It's written with sparkly pens. And on the back of this note, there are some notes about the latest mystery that the Secret Mystery Club is investigating."

Billie's mouth drops open.

She was in such a hurry to write the note that morning that she forgot to turn to a new page!

Mrs. Singh laughs. "It's all right. No one else knows," she says, smiling. "Your secret is safe with me.

And actually, your club is partly the reason I called you into my office today. I was hoping you might be able to look into something for me?"

Billie looks at the others, who are as surprised as she is.

She grins. "Sure! What is it?"

"Well," says Mrs. Singh, leaning closer to them and lowering her voice, "I happen to know that there is a secret time capsule hidden in this school somewhere."

Billie gasps.

Mrs. Singh smiles and continues. "It must be a hundred years old now. Almost as old as the school itself. But the original plans for the building were lost a long time ago. I have always wanted to find that time capsule, but I'm much too busy to look for it myself. What do you say? Is this a mystery you'd be willing to look into?"

Billie feels her tummy **flip** around with excitement.

She doesn't even have to look at her friends to know they are feeling the same way.

"We'd love to!" she says. "Wouldn't we?" She turns to face Jack, Mika and Alex, who nod happily.

"Wonderful!" says Mrs. Singh. "But this is our secret for now, all right? I want to surprise the rest of the school when we find it."

"Of course!" Billie says seriously. "We'll get to work right away."

She looks back at the others. Alex, Mika and Jack all look as happy as she feels. The Secret Mystery Club is back in business. And this time with a real, actual, **grown-up** mystery to solve. Billie can't wait to get started!

To be continued...

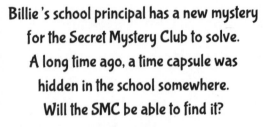